SLEEPING
BEAUTY

Once upon a time there was a King and Queen who had a daughter. The fairies of the land had bestowed many gifts on her; beauty, charm, and a kind, generous nature. But there was a wicked old fairy who had a grudge against the King and Queen, and was most annoyed that she hadn't been invited to the christening.

"One day", she muttered, looking at the little girl,

"you will cut your finger on a spinning-wheel and you will die".

"No!" said a good fairy, who had overheard the wicked words. "The girl will not die, she will sleep for a hundred years. She will be woken up by a handsome young prince and will then go on living as though nothing had happened."

When the King heard of the bad fairy's prophecy, he was most alarmed and immediately made a new law. "Under pain of death," the law said, "it is forbidden for anyone to own a spinning-wheel."

And to make sure, the King had burnt every spinning-wheel in the land.

And so the years passed. When the princess was fifteen, she went, one morning, up into a disused tower in the palace. To her surprise, she found there an old woman who was spinning at a wheel.

The old woman received the princess kindly enough and when the girl asked to work the wheel on her own, the old woman let her. But the princess cut her finger on the wheel and immediately she fell to the ground as if in a swoon. The bad fairy's prophecy had come true.

"She's sleeping," said the King, when he was brought to the tower. "Take her to her room." But the King was wrong. The princess would sleep for a hundred years.

At that moment, the good fairy appeared. With a wave of her wand, she put to sleep the King, the Queen, the courtiers, the cooks, the servants, and all the animals and birds that lived or

moved in or around the palace. That was the best she could do to counter the wicked fairy's spell, for now everyone would wake up at the same time as the princess.

And so all life stopped at the palace. Only the trees continued to grow and so high and so thick did they become that the palace was almost hidden from view behind the foliage.

A hundred years passed, and everything remained the same. One day, a young prince was out hunting in the forest and he happened to see through a gap in the trees the towers of the sleeping palace.

Curious, he pushed his way through the thick greenery and could hardly believe his eyes when he saw all the motionless figures.

When he came upon the sleeping princess, he gave a cry of wonder at her beauty and touched her face with his hand.

Immediately the spell was broken. The princess woke up, and with her the King, the Queen, the guards, the cooks, the servants, the birds, the dogs, and the cats.

It was a time for great rejoicing, and a huge banquet was prepared. The prince and the princess were married, and eventually they became King and Queen and lived happily ever after.

PUSS
IN
BOOTS

Once upon a time there was a miller who had three sons. When he died he left his mill to his eldest son, his donkey to his second son but all his youngest son received was a cat! "Don't worry," said this remarkable cat to his young master, "you wait and see — you will be best off in the end. Just give me a pair of boots and let me go away for a while." Puss in Boots set off next morning and, on his travels, found a rabbit in a snare. He took it along with him to the royal palace where he told the King that it was a present from his master, the Marquis of Carabas.

The King was delighted and, later on, Puss brought him two partridges — again from his master. Then Puss learnt that the King and Princess would be passing a nearby river so he told his master to throw away his clothes and jump in. "But I can't swim!" said his master. "So much the better," said Puss. "Hurry! The King is coming." His master plunged into the river and, as the King drew near, Puss cried, "Help! My master, the Marquis of Carabas is drowning!" The King ordered his men to jump in and save the Marquis and he even provided some fine clothes for him.

He looked so handsome in his new clothes that the Princess found him very attractive. "You must join us in our carriage," said the King. "I want to thank you for your gifts." Meanwhile, Puss in Boots set off again.

As he went through the fields he said to some peasants,
"If you don't say these lands belong to the Marquis of
Carabas you will be killed!" The peasants said they would
obey.

Further on, Puss in Boots came to a giant's castle. The giant was the real owner of the surrounding lands. Puss began to talk to him and flatter him. He asked if the giant could change himself into different creatures. "Of course I can!" said the giant.

"Change yourself into a lion," said Puss and the giant at once became a roaring lion.

"Now change yourself into a mouse," said Puss. The giant did so and at once Puss pounced on him and gobbled him up! Now Puss went to meet the royal party and he was able to tell them that the castle and lands belonged to his rich master, the Marquis of Carabas.

The King congratulated the Marquis on his clever servant Puss in Boots and they all went into the castle where a feast was prepared. The King offered his daughter's hand in marriage to the Marquis who was delighted to accept. When they were married Puss in Boots was made Chief Courtier in their palace!

SNOW-WHITE
AND ROSE-RED

Do you know the story of the two little girls, Snow-White and Rose-Red who lived with their mother at the edge of a large forest? I will tell it to you.

When Snow-White and Rose-Red went to gather strawberries and mushrooms the forest deer did not run away at their approach. Even the birds flew round them and took the twigs which the little girls offered them. It was such fun! The squirrels and the rabbits were also friendly with them. Snow-White and Rose-Red were not afraid to go for a walk in the woods at night and occasionally they even slept under a tree. You might think this was rather foolish and that they would have been better off in their own little bed but nothing ever happened to them.

One morning the brightness of the sun's rays woke them up and they were alarmed to find that they had been asleep on the edge of a deep precipice. Fortunately their guardian-angel had watched over them and he wished them well before he left.

Time passed and winter came. The little girls no longer left their house. A little lamb kept them company. One evening, during a snow-storm, there was a knock at the cottage door. Rose-Red opened it and uttered a great cry of fright when she saw before her an enormous brown bear.

"Please let me in," he said, "I'm dying of cold and I've had nothing to eat for two days."

What would you have done in their place? It was very hard to keep him out and shut the door in his face. Their mother was kind-hearted and she took pity on him.

"Come in, Mr. Bear," she said. "Come and get warm. We were just going to have a meal."

"Thank you very much, madam," he replied and came inside.

It's rather unusual to entertain a bear to dinner and their mother seemed a little embarrassed by her strange visitor.

The little girls, who were very nervous at first, soon felt a little braver. They came up to the bear smiling.

"You have a lovely fur coat," they said. "It's so thick!"

"I need it," he replied, "because this year the winter is so severe."

The bear did not leave the house before Spring.

When the fine weather returned he went away after thanking his hostesses for their kind hospitality. It seemed very empty in the cottage and the little girls often thought about their friend the bear and looked forward to seeing him the following winter.

He had promised to return to them.

One day Snow-White and Rose-Red were gathering strawberries in the wood when they saw a little dwarf in difficulties.

"Why don't you help me?" he cried. "Can't you see my beard is caught in this tree-trunk? I'm a prisoner!"

What should they do? Then Rose-Red had an idea.

"Pass me the scissors from the basket," she said to her sister. "I'm going to cut a piece off his beard."

Clip! Clip! This was soon done and the dwarf was free.

Do you think he said thank-you to the little girls! Not at all! He was extremely angry, clenched his fists and glared at them! "You've spoilt my beard!" he cried. "What a disaster! It will never grow as fine as it was before. Just see what you've done! I was so proud of my beard."

He went on and on until the two little girls could hardly believe their ears.

Several days later they met the little dwarf again. His fishing-line, to which was attached a large fish, was caught in his beard and he was in great danger of falling into the river.

What could they do? Clip! Clip! Just what they did on the previous occasion. The beard was cut, the fish disappeared and the dwarf was saved. Just as before he raged at them, waving his arms and speaking crossly about the scissors and the little girls. What a peculiar little man!

But that wasn't all. Sometime later the little girls saw the dwarf filling a sack with precious stones.

"Go away!" he cried in a fury and he would have struck them but, just then, the bear appeared.

"You wretched creature!" said the bear. "So this is how you repay their kindness. Very well then — this is what you deserve!" He dealt the dwarf a great blow on the head and knocked him down the precipice!

Then, all at once, before the astonished gaze of the little girls, the bear changed into a handsome prince! You can quess what followed. The prince married Snow-White and his brother married Rose-Red.

Their mother went to live with them in the castle and they all lived happily ever after.

ASS'S SKIN

Once upon a time there was a kingdom where everybody was happy. The King ruled wisely and he had no enemies. Everyone had enough to eat and the days slipped by quite peacefully. The Queen was so beautiful and so kind that all the people loved her. To add to their great happiness a pretty princess was born and she grew lovelier each year.

In the magnificent palace where the royal family lived there was one thing which visitors found surprising and that was the great respect shown to an ass who lived in a room next to the throne-room. Of course he was no ordinary ass — each morning the King found a bag of gold pieces in his stable. No wonder the ass was so well-guarded by the King's best palace sentries.

Then one day ill-fortune struck the palace — just as the rain follows the fine weather. The Queen fell ill with a mysterious illness and died.

Before she died she said to her husband, "If you want to marry again when I am gone you will marry only a woman who is more beautiful and more wise than I am." The King, his eyes filled with tears, promised to obey her instructions. After several months of mourning he thought he would marry again but he could not find anyone in his kingdom — or in the neighbouring kingdoms, who surpassed his late wife in beauty and charm. He became quite mad with grief, and wanted only to die.

In his madness he demanded that his daughter marry a neighbouring prince, and rule with him in the King's place. But the princess did not want to, and she asked her fairy godmother for help.

"We must gain time," said the godmother. "Tell your father you will agree only if he gives you a dress the colour of the sun."

The King ordered the finest tailors in the kingdom to make the dress out of gold silk embroidered with diamonds.

Seven days later the dress was exhibited before the court. It made quite a sensation and the princess did not know what to say next but her godmother came to her aid. "Your father owns an ass which regularly supplies heaps of gold pieces. Demand that he give you the animal's skin. He is sure to refuse and then he will have to give up the idea of this marriage."

But, contrary to her predictions, the skin was offered to the princess. "It's useless!" she cried and burst into tears. Fortunately the fairy had another idea.

"There is no need to be afraid, what we are doing is in a good cause. Pull yourself together and we'll arrange for you to run away. You can disguise yourself in the ass's skin and smear your face with ashes. Nobody would believe that such an ugly creature was really a princess. However, take my magic wand with you so that, when you wish, you can regain your former appearance."

In this way the princess escaped from the palace before dawn. As she wandered sadly along the road the King, in great distress, went looking for her in the palace.

However, by this time the princess was a long way off and she ended up at a farm where they needed a girl to look after the pigs.

She was tormented by the other servants who called her 'Ass's Skin' and they made fun of her. Only on Sundays did she get a little peace. Then she retired to her little room, cleaned herself up and then took out the magic wand. From her casket she also took out her magnificent jewels. When she had adorned herself she looked in the mirror. The pleasure of seeing herself so beautiful again helped to make up for her great sorrows.

Now it happened that a young prince, returning from the hunt, stopped in the farmyard and, catching sight of the lovely young girl, was astonished by her beauty. Night and day he thought about her and wanted to see her again so he returned to the farm but, when he asked about her, nobody knew of any lovely young girl.

"There is only Ass's Skin here and she is an ugly old hag!" The prince went home and he was so upset that he lost his appetite and never wanted to see anyone

again. His mother was heartbroken and asked him what was wrong. He told her that the only thing that would make him happy would be a cake made for him by Ass's Skin. So, by order of the Queen, Ass's Skin made the cake with the finest flour, butter, and eggs. As she mixed it one of her rings fell into the mixture and when the prince ate the cake he almost swallowed the gold ring! Upon finding it his heart swelled with joy but next morning his melancholy returned.

"I will marry the girl whose finger that ring will fit," he declared.

"Very well," said his mother.

The news was spread around and young girls of all classes and kinds came to the palace. One after the other each tried to make the ring go on her finger but in vain. No-one seemed to have a hand that was slim enough.

Princesses, countesses, baronesses — all presented their hands but their fingers were too fat. Milliners, dress-makers, lacemakers — they all came but the ring would not fit. After the servants came the cooks and the scullery-maids and at last they got down to Ass's Skin.

Covered with the skin she approached the prince and, despite her dreadful clothes, he saw that she was very beautiful and then he recognised her!

He slipped the ring on her finger and said he would marry her at once! The princess's father, now quite recovered, hastened to the wedding with her godmother, so there was nothing to spoil the young couple's happiness.

THE MUSICIANS OF BREMEN

Once upon a time there was an ass who was growing too old to work and his master was going to get rid of him.

Poor thing! What would become of him? He went away, very sad indeed, to look for a lodging. On the way he met a dog, a cat and a cock who were in the same sad predicament. They had a consultation and discussed how they could get out of their difficulties. After some reflection they decided to become musicians. Boom! Boom! Tra-la-la! Music was delightful to listen to and musicians were well paid. Everybody liked them — there was no better occupation — so they decided to go to Bremen where they thought they would easily find work.

It was a long way to Bremen. They climbed hills, crossed plains, waded through streams and, one evening, they arrived at a large wood.

"I can go no further," declared the cock. "This is where I'm going to spend the night," and he settled down on the branch of a tree. From there he could see a little light and the four friends decided to make one final effort. They went towards the light and soon found themselves in the middle of a clearing before a small house. Smoke was coming out of the little chimney.

"Be very careful," said the dog. "I don't like the look of this!" So they approached noiselessly and the ass looked through the window. He adjusted his glasses because he was rather short-sighted and his companions, who were growing impatient, begged him to say what he could see.

They hoisted themselves up beside him and looked inside.
"Hush!" said the ass, "there are several . . ."
"Several what?"
"I think they are robbers — at least they look like them."
"What are they doing?"
"They are getting some delicious food ready to eat."
"That's just what we need!" said the dog.

"I have a plan," said the ass. "Let the dog jump on my back, then the cat jump on the dog's back, then the cock stand on the cat's head."

No sooner said than done — then came the music. The ass leapt forward carrying his companions and at the risk of losing his glasses.

Bang! Crash! The window flew into pieces and the animals burst out into fearsome cries. The robbers threw up their arms in alarm and one fell over backwards.

"They've found our hide-out!" they said.

The candle went out and the animals howled louder and louder. The robbers did not hesitate. Frightened to death they fled from the scene. Naturally the ass, the dog the cat and the cock thoroughly enjoyed their meal.

During the night the robbers, being now a little calmer, came back to prowl around their house, curious to know who their visitors were and what they were doing.

The boldest among them decided to go inside.

"They must be asleep," he said. "There is no noise."

He never forgot what happened after that — it's a wonder he was not killed.

Yowl! The cat scratched his face, the dog bit his legs, the ass kicked him and the cock pecked his head and he was thrown roughly out of the door.

The robber told his tale to his companions.

"I risked my life!" he declared. "I shall never set foot in this awful place again!" And the others followed his advice.

From then onwards the ass, the dog, the cat and the cock lived peacefully in the cottage in the middle of the forest and there they stayed happily for the rest of their lives, playing music for everyone to enjoy.

THE QUEEN
OF THE SNOWS

Everybody knows that the devil is a wicked person who goes about doing evil. One day, when he had nothing else to do, he invented an extraordinary mirror. People who were beautiful looked ugly in it, happy people saw themselves as miserable and everybody felt sad. The devil was very pleased and told all his friends about it. They said, "Yes — it's wonderful! There's nothing like it in the whole world!" And the devil felt very proud.

"But I have a better idea!" he said. "I'm going to try out my mirror on human beings. I think it will be great fun!" "Bravo!" exclaimed his friends. Now the devil hates goodness and happiness so he called to his imps and told them to go down to Earth with the mirror and show it to men, women and children. All these people immediately became sad and unhappy. The imps then dashed round the sky looking for the angels but they dropped the mirror which broke into a thousand pieces. These fragments covered the whole Earth.

A little girl called Gerda and a little boy called Kay lived in the same town. They were poor but that didn't prevent them from being happy. One day a fragment of the mirror flew into Kay's eyes and he became wicked. He grumbled and bullied poor little Gerda all the time. Then he decided to go and fasten his sledge behind that of the Snow Queen who was gliding through the sky. The Queen let him sit beside her and they started their long voyage. Gerda was left behind — very sad.

Gerda missed her friend Kay so much. One day she decided to go and find him, even if she had to travel to the Ice Palace of the Snow Queen. She asked everyone she met if they had seen her friend, but no one could help her.

Summer turned into autumn, and the leaves were falling from the trees, but still Gerda kept on searching. She walked and walked and each day grew colder. Winter was coming.

Then the winter came. Snow settled on the trees in the forest and covered the ground. As Gerda wandered on she met an owl. "Hullo, little girl!" he exclaimed. "What are you doing all by yourself in the wood?"

"I'm looking for my friend Kay," she replied.

"I've seen a young boy accompanied by a princess. He was going to be married," said the owl. "Perhaps he was your young friend."

"Show me where to find them," requested Gerda.

She walked for days before she reached the palace where the princess lived, but she was very disappointed when she found the young husband wasn't Kay. The princess took pity on her and gave her a reindeer to help her on her journey. They set off and travelled many miles.

Eventually they arrived in Finland. The reindeer was tired, so they were glad when a kind Finnish lady said they could rest in her little house.

The reindeer had lots of hay to eat and Gerda became friends with a Finnish girl. The Finnish lady cooked a delicious meal.

When Gerda had rested she was ready to continue her journey. If only she could find her friend Kay!

She asked if anyone had seen him, but just as before no one knew of a young man, or where the Ice Queen's Palace might be.

Gerda and the reindeer sped on across the land. Spring came, and at last the weather became warmer. But Kay was nowhere to be found. Each night kind Northerners looked after Gerda and her brave reindeer. But no one could help them in their search.

Eventually they came to Lapland in the far north, where it is never dark in Summer. There they saw the Aurora Borealis shining like shimmering curtains in the sky.

The Laplanders asked what brought Gerda to their distant land, but when they were asked about Kay and the Ice Queen they shook their heads.

"No, we have seen no young boy. Good luck with your journey!" They waved goodbye and Gerda and the reindeer went on their way.

At last Gerda and the reindeer travelled so far that there were no people at all to ask.

Then one day Gerda saw a beautiful palace made entirely from ice and she realised that she had reached the palace of the Ice Queen. Bravely she went inside.

Gerda was very frightened because it was so cold in the palace. The walls glistened with frost and the icicles tinkled in the chilly breeze. Could Kay really be here, she wondered.

Suddenly she saw her friend Kay. He was waiting on the
Queen of the Ice. Gerda whispered to him how much his
friends missed him. Kay began to weep, and the splinter fell
from his eye. "I want to go home," he cried.

In no time the reindeer carried both the children home.
How glad their friends were to see them!

Pinocchio

One day Gepetto the old carpenter decided to make a puppet. When he tried to shape the nose he ran into trouble. He tried to shorten it but it still stayed long. Then — to his surprise — the puppet started to laugh and to move its arms and legs.

"What shall I do with you?" asked Gepetto.

"I want to go to school," replied Pinocchio.

The old man agreed and bought him his school outfit.

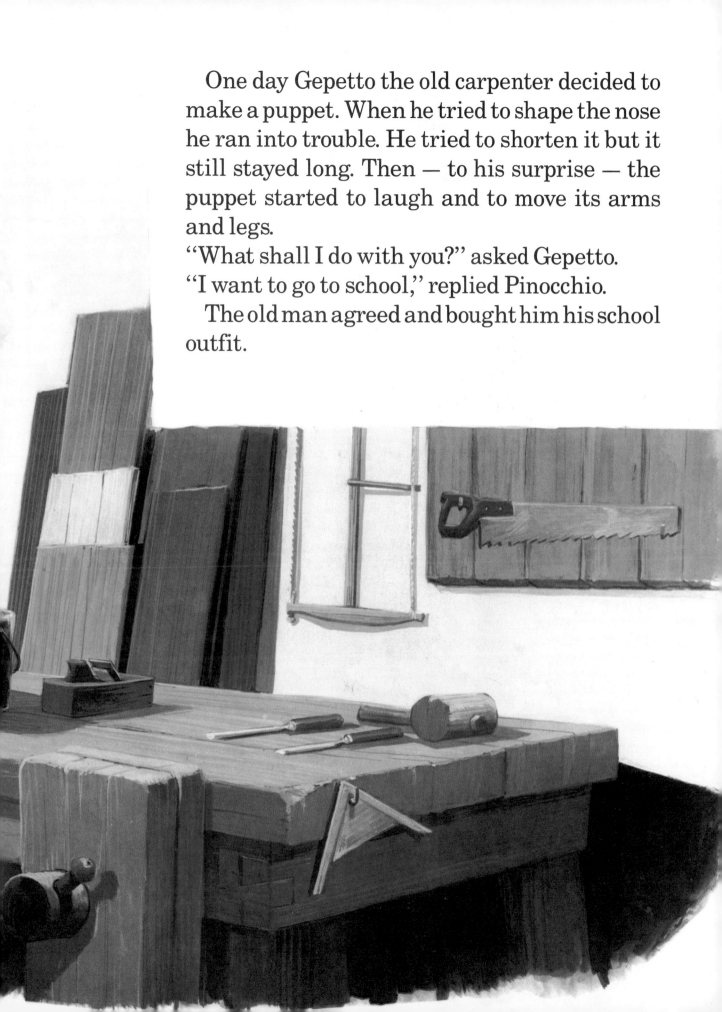

Pinocchio set off but on the way he came to a puppet theatre. Two of the actors saw him and put him on the stage but he caused such an upset that the director threw him out! Pinocchio wept and told him about poor Gepetto so the director gave him five gold pieces to take home to his father.

Pinocchio went happily on his way and eventually he met a lame fox and a blind cat. He showed them his gold pieces. "I know a way to double those!" said the fox. "Follow us to the Land of Fools." They walked together till nightfall and then Pinocchio realised that his companions intended to steal his gold so he slipped the pieces into his mouth and ran off. Unfortunately their legs were better than his so they caught him and decided to hang him on a tree until he agreed to open his mouth.

A fairy saw what had happened and sent her falcon to set him free. When he had recovered the fairy said: "Where are your gold pieces?" "I've lost them", said Pinocchio. As soon as he told this lie his nose grew so long that it reached the wall. But the kind fairy ordered a woodpecker to shorten it again.

"I want to be a good boy," said Pinocchio.
"In that case you must do as you are told and work hard," said the fairy. Alas! Pinocchio allowed himself to be taken off by some young scoundrels. They went to the Land of Sport in a carriage drawn by twelve asses. When they reached there Pinocchio played all the time but, one morning, he and his friends woke up and found themselves covered with grey hair and they had long asses' ears. It was a great shock!

Pinocchio was sold to a man who wanted his skin for a drum. The man first threw him in the sea to drown him but the fishes ate the ass's skin off him and he came out again as a wooden puppet. "Thank you very much," said Pinocchio swimming happily around.

Just then a huge mouth opened in front of him and he was swallowed up by an enormous fish. In the darkness he saw a light and, as he drew near he saw that it was old Gepetto sitting near a lighted candle. He threw himself into the old man's arms with great joy.

"We must try to swim out," said Pinocchio.
"Hold on to me," said Gepetto. "Then we can get out together." Before long they were safely on the seashore. As a result of his adventures Pinocchio became a real little boy. He never left his father again, he made sure he always told the truth, and he always worked hard at school.

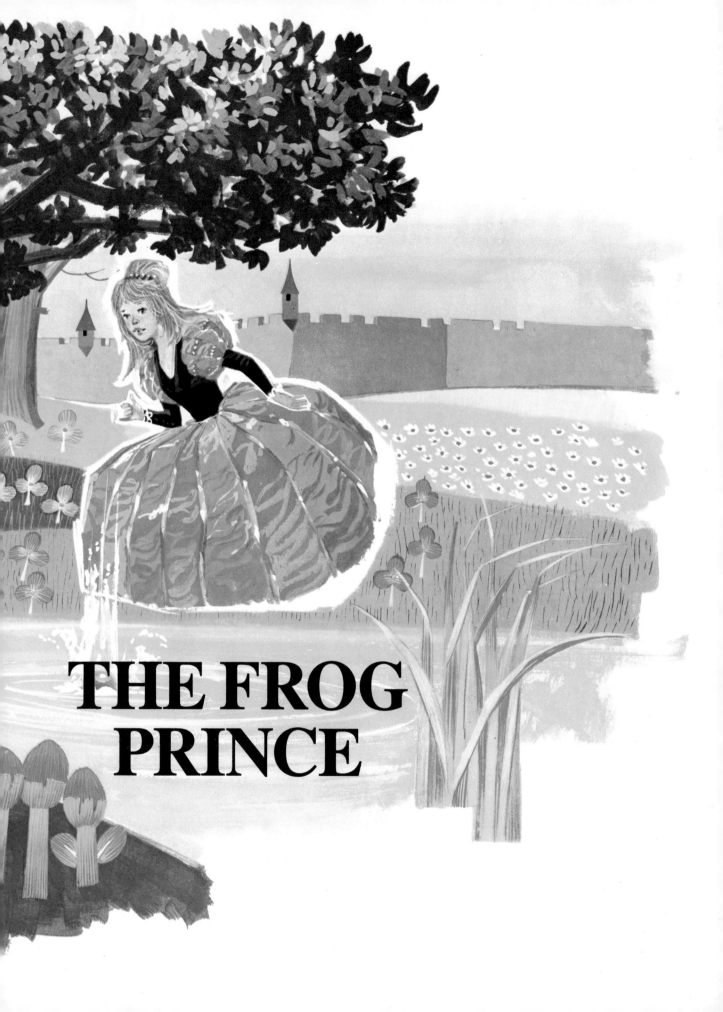

THE FROG
PRINCE

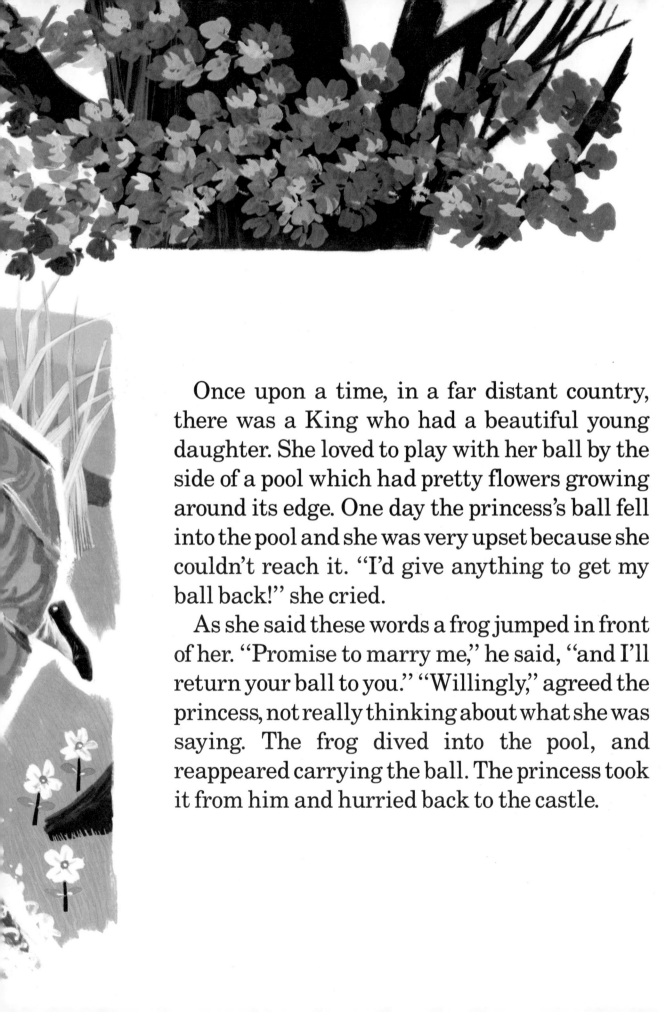

Once upon a time, in a far distant country, there was a King who had a beautiful young daughter. She loved to play with her ball by the side of a pool which had pretty flowers growing around its edge. One day the princess's ball fell into the pool and she was very upset because she couldn't reach it. "I'd give anything to get my ball back!" she cried.

As she said these words a frog jumped in front of her. "Promise to marry me," he said, "and I'll return your ball to you." "Willingly," agreed the princess, not really thinking about what she was saying. The frog dived into the pool, and reappeared carrying the ball. The princess took it from him and hurried back to the castle.

But the next day, whilst she was sitting with her father, the King, a strange visitor was announced. It was the frog — and he had come to claim her! The King frowned as he listened to all the explanations. "Very well," he said finally, "you made a promise — you must keep it. You shall marry the frog!" The young girl went up to her room weeping with rage.

To her horror she saw the frog sitting beside her bed.

"Go away, you wicked frog!" she cried. "I never want to see you again." The frog went sadly into a corner of the room and sat watching her with large reproachful eyes. He sighed so much that at last the princess asked him: "Why do you want to marry me? You are too ugly to be my husband. Wouldn't you be better off in the pool where you live?"

"No," replied the frog sadly. "You are so beautiful — and I'm sure you are kind as well. All I want is to live near you and hear your lovely voice. Your eyes are like stars — I can't help wanting to see them. If you reject me I'll die!"

The young girl was touched by the frog's devotion. "You seem to be really in love with me," she said. "Don't you realise that I have quite a bad reputation? I'm most disobedient to my father — perhaps it is partly because

I have no mother. However, if you wish, you may stay here and help me to become as beautiful and kind as you seem to think I am." And she smiled at the frog and offered him her hand.

Then a most extraordinary thing happened. A bright light seemed to dazzle her eyes and she suddenly saw before her a handsome young man who smiled at her and kissed her hand. "May I thank you most sincerely," he said. "As a

result of your kindness I am no longer an ugly frog but I have regained my original form. I am Prince Kindheart. A wicked fairy changed me into a frog. Now I will stay with you forever — if you will accept me as your husband."

The princess delighted, clapped her hands. "We must go at once to my father," she said. "I can't wait to present my fiancé!" Everybody was astounded at the wonderful

miracle that had been performed. Soon, all the bells in the kingdom rang out for the wedding of the princess and Prince Kindheart. The young couple went for a tour around the kingdom in a carriage drawn by four white horses.

"Our princess has become as good as she is beautiful," said the people as they saw her go by. "Thanks to the Frog Prince," they added.

They lived happily ever afterwards and had lots of children, as beautiful as their mother and as kind as their father.

The Goose Girl

High on a mountain, in a little cottage hidden among the bushes, lived an old woman who was lame and had to walk with a crutch. She was a witch and, although she was very old, she still went out gathering herbs, kneeling on the ground, and picking apples and pears to fill two huge baskets. One morning a young man came by just as the old woman had finished and she asked him if he would be good enough to carry her basket home for her.

The young man was the son of a count but he gladly agreed to take the heavy baskets and, followed by the witch, he set off to climb the narrow mountain paths. "Shall we stop and have a rest?" he asked, but the old woman refused. "My house is still a long way off and, if we stop, we shan't arrive before nightfall."

So saying, she jumped onto the young man's shoulders. He nearly fell over, but carried on walking without a word.

Finally they got to the old woman's hut. On the threshold was a very ugly young girl, who was tending a flock of geese.

When the old woman jumped to the ground, the young count, exhausted, lay down on the bench under the window

and fell into a deep sleep.

When he woke up early the next morning, the old woman was holding out an emerald box, which shone like a thousand fires.

"This is your reward," she said. "Take good care of it!"

The young man thanked the witch and continued on his way to the neighbouring kingdom.

His journey took him to a royal palace where he called on the King and Queen to pay his respects and he presented the Queen with the emerald box. The Queen opened the box and saw there a pearl. She began to weep because it resembled the tears her young daughter had shed when the King had banished her from his kingdom. The King had thought, wrongly, that his little daughter did not love him as much as his other daughters did. Now he was sorry for what he had done and, acting on the young man's advice, the King and Queen decided to go and consult the witch.

That evening, when the girl arrived with the geese, the old woman sent her to the well in the bushes at the bottom of the valley. The girl washed herself and the ugliness seemed to be washed away from her face!

Looking into the water, she saw that she was quite beautiful with long fair hair. However, she still felt sad and tears like pearls fell from her eyes. A sudden stir among the trees made her jump and she ran off. At the same, time the ugliness returned to her face.

When she arrived home the old woman said to her: "It is three years since you came here. Your time is over — you must tidy yourself up and go away. We have to part."

"But where can I go?" asked the young girl in tears.

"Don't worry," said the witch, "just do as I say and your face will become beautiful again. Go and put on the dress you wore when you first came here."

Meanwhile the King and Queen were trying to find the witch, helped by the young man. One night he caught sight of a young girl looking at herself in the well by moonlight.

Unfortunately she must have heard him moving about in the trees and she fled — but he had recognised her as the goose-girl! He ran to tell the King and Queen what he had seen and they all three set off for the house on the mountain.

They knocked at the little window and the witch invited them into her clean and shining little house. "You were unkind to banish your daughter," she said to the King, "but I think you have been punished enough!" Then she called the young girl, who was really the princess, and she arrived looking as pretty as an angel. She threw herself into her parents' arms and they all cried with joy.

"What would you like me to give you, to make amends, my poor child?", asked the King.

"She needs nothing," said the witch smiling. "I am giving her my little house and all the tears of pearl she has wept for you." Then she disappeared. Her poor dwelling changed into a beautiful palace full of servants. The white geese became pretty young girls who attended the princess when she married the young count.

The Princess and the Pea

Once upon a time there was a young prince who wanted to get married, but he wanted his wife to be a princess, a real princess. So he went out to look for one. He went by land and sea and he went all the way around the world. He found there were plenty of princesses, but he could never be sure they were real ones.

So where was the girl who would make him a perfect wife, the beautiful, gentle, good princess he dreamed of?

"You're a difficult customer," said a King who he had gone to see one day. "My daughter is a pearl beyond price; look at her, talk to her. If you do not fall in love with her, you will never find the person you are looking for, you have my word for it as a King."

This girl had a delightful smile and was very pretty. The problem was that she waddled like a goose and she made fun of her courtiers all the time. The prince thought that she could not possibly be a real princess.

Once again, the prince went off even sadder than he had been before. He was getting tired of looking for the princess of his dreams and not finding her, and finally he took the road home again. "I'm going home alone," he thought, "What will my parents think?"

Still feeling disappointed, the young man came in sight of his town. Alas! It was a joyless return, but the King and Queen tried hard to make their son forget his sadness.

Life went back to normal, until one evening there was a
violent storm. The doors and windows of the palace were all
closed and everyone was glad they weren't out on a night like
this. All of a sudden, they heard a knocking on the main gate.
"It's just the wind," said the Queen.
"I'm not sure it is," said the King. And he went to open the
door himself. A beautiful young girl was standing on the
doorstep.

"Who are you?" asked the King.
"I'm a princess," she replied. "I was caught out in the storm and I got lost."
"Come in, you poor child," said the King. "We'll look after you." The prince thought the young stranger was very beautiful, and was bound to be a real princess. "I'll find out whether she's telling the truth," thought the Queen.

Without saying anything, the Queen went into the bedroom. She lifted the bedding and put a little pea on the bed. Then she piled twenty-one mattresses on top. She offered the bed to the girl, who accepted it gratefully because she was very tired.

The next day, they asked her whether she had slept well. "No, I'm afraid I didn't," she replied. "There was something hard under my mattress, I'm black and blue this morning. I couldn't get a wink of sleep!"

She had passed the test. Only a real princess would have been so delicate that she could feel a pea through twenty-one layers of mattress. The Queen decked out the princess in one of her finest dresses, arranged her hair and placed a garland of pearls on her head. When the prince saw her again, he fell in love straight away and asked the princess to marry him. When the marriage took place there were great celebrations and everyone was very happy ever after.